A Moose With a Uke

by Aaron Risi

ISBN: 978-1-6847-0340-1 (sc)
ISBN: 978-1-6847-0339-5 (e)

Library of Congress Control Number: 2019906720

This book is dedicated to all those who have a desire to learn. Pass on knowledge gained and we grow together as a global community.

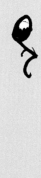

A Moose With a Uke

by Aaron Risi

The ukulele has brought me so much happiness. Practicing and learning are fun and challenging.
—*Monty the Moose*

Hi! I'm Monty. Thanks for stopping by!

I live in Harmony Grove, a giant forest at the base of Hope Rock. This is the story about how I got my uke.

On a bright sunny day,
in a forest far away.

At the entrance of the forest, there was an old bridge that crossed the river. A mischievous cloud passed by, sent a gust of wind toward the bus, and caused it to tip.

The trunk on the roof broke free, fell into the river, and was washed away in an instant.

"Hey, Sonny, there's something in the river," I said.

Sonny replied, "Wake me up if it's anything good."

I was half way
down the hill before
Sonny began to chase after me.
Both of us yelled out,
"Save that trunk before
it goes over the falls!"

Professor Wiseman exclaimed,
"Great job saving the trunk, boys. If it went
over the falls, it would have been destroyed!"

Looks like it's filled with an assortment of instruments:
a banjo, ukulele, upright bass, fiddle, and an acoustic guitar. "What an opportunity!
Learning how to play an instrument is a valuable skill—one that can last a lifetime."

"Travel near and far, and you'll see by playing and enjoying music with others that music is a common language. Go ahead. Choose one, Monty."

Excited, I selected the ukulele.

Professor Wiseman explained, "Originally from the island of Hawaii, the four-stringed instrument is played by strumming the strings in an up-and-down pattern."

Sonny chose the fiddle. As he reached for it, he found a note that said,
> *To whomever finds this trunk full of instruments: Please learn to play them!*
> *Have fun! Please return them when done--if you can find me :)*

Professor Wiseman said, "Let's do what the note says and try them out! You picked the fiddle, Sonny. It is played by placing it under the chin and using a bow to glide across the strings."

We played a duet with our instruments and created sounds and melodies that carried across the pond and into the heart of the forest.

Mr. Arthur was out that morning when he heard the music coming from the trees.

He poked his head through to the clearing to see Sonny and me playing for the creatures of the pond.

Mr. Arthur asked angrily, "What's that? Music? Where did you boys get those instruments?"

Professor Wiseman explained, "They were in this trunk the boys pulled out of the river, Mr. Arthur.

It's a good thing they were here.

The instruments would have been destroyed by the falls had they gone over."

Mr. Arthur said,
"We should try and locate their owner.
In the meantime, do you mind if I join you?"

I replied, "Not at all! Select an instrument, and jump in! Or should I say, hop in!"

At the same time, Doris Delores was out for a swim when she heard the music.

"Morning, everyone. I'm Doris Delores. I swam over to get a closer look to see where the music was coming from. Do you mind if I sit and listen for a while?"

Sonny replied, "Forget listening! Why not join us?"

"I thought you'd never ask," said Doris Delores.

Doris Delores grabbed the banjo, a five-string instrument. She was a fast learner and took to it like an expert.

Mr. Arthur selected the upright bass.

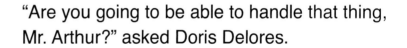

"Are you going to be able to handle that thing, Mr. Arthur?" asked Doris Delores.

Mr. Arthur lifted up the bass, hopped up onto a tree stump, and replied, "Of course! I'm ready!"

We practiced together, learning all we could. Professor Wiseman instructed each one of us. "Keep practicing, and then practice some more!"

Doris Delores said, "I just remembered that I saw a bus with a trunk like this one tied to the roof earlier."

"Actually, I spotted that bus making its way through the center of the forest just before I got here," added Professor Wiseman. "Let's follow the bus, and we'll catch up to it before it leaves the forest," I said.

We chased the bus around for the rest of the afternoon and tried to catch up to it. Every time we reached a point where the bus had been, we were told we'd just missed it.

As we neared Hope Rock, we saw it crest over the horizon. Hope Rock is a strange and mysterious place. Those who know about it speak of its powers of inspiration. The clouds hide the top. I've heard that if you climb halfway up, you can see beyond the edge of the forest. What if you scaled it to the peak, above the clouds? Who knows what's up there?

We spotted the bus parked at the base of Hope Rock and sang out in joy because we'd finally managed to catch up to it. We made our way to the driver's side of the van. The driver tried to introduce himself, but before he could, Mr. Arthur blurted out, "You're Vince Hairdo!"

Doris Delores asked, "The rock star?"

Vince Hairdo replied, "The one and only!"

"I noticed I lost the trunk when I stopped to set up camp," said Vince Hairdo. "I drove around and looked for it. Then I realized it fell off when I crossed that rickety bridge."

I said, "We saved the trunk from the falls and followed the instructions on the note that said to learn to play the instruments. Along the way, we had an adventure and became a band."

Vince replied, "I've been collecting the instruments for a long time. I wrote the note in case the trunk was ever lost. I think that old trunk has a little magic. It found its way to you! I've carried those instruments around, not knowing who they'd end up with—now I do! Monty, I'd like you and the Harmony Grove String Band to keep the instruments and use them to start a new journey!"

Vince said, "I'm feeling inspired being at Hope Rock. Would you four like to join me for my concert?"

The group replied, "Yes!"

Vince said, "Thanks for jamming with me. I've always wanted to pass these instruments on. I'm happy your group will use them to make new melodies and entertain the next generation. Keep practicing and traveling to new places! New friends and adventures await. As long as you're willing, they'll seek you out."

As I stood there and watched the bus drive off into the sunset, Doris Delores walked up, put her arm around me, and said, "I'm sure that's not the last time we'll see that guy."
" I think uke are right, Doris Delores!" I replied.

For more with Monty and friends, visit AMoosewithaUke.com.

Monty's Song

Words & Music by Aaron Risi

Monty's Song

Special Thanks

Mom thanks for bringing my vision to life! I couldn't have done it without you!

Special thanks to my wife Ali and my daughter Grace for your support and patience!

Contributors

Jean MacDonald - Marketing Director
For more information about Jean MacDonald: jeanconnects.com

Leslie Lipps - Website and Graphic Design
For more information about Leslie Lipps: leslielipps.com

Thanks to Tim Schoch, Greg Thom, Ben Griffin, Melissa Riddle, Alice Lipps, Dean McClements, Tee Arsenault and Pete Labourdette of petesguitarstudio.com.

Yo Arty, Thanks!

A Moose with a Uke

Welcome to Harmony Grove!!